May you always
believe in the
magic of fairy tales.

Michelle Eastman

For Logan - My favorite fairy tale began the day you were born.
With love and thanks to Aunt Agnes and my entire family.
"Above all else, guard your heart, for everything you do flows from it."
(Proverbs 4:23)
-MRE

For my wonderful wife, Ashleigh, and our two amazing sons, Kyan and
Travis, and for Mom and Dad - thank you all for your endless love
and support. You guys are the best.
-KFR

Fonts used: 'BudBird' by John David and 'Henny Penny' by Brownfox

ISBN: 978-0-9916244-4-7
Library of Congress Control Number: 2015901918

Byway Press, USA

DUST FAIRY TALES
ABSOLUTELY AGGIE

Written by
Michelle R. Eastman

Illustrated by
Kevin Richter

Do you know what happens,
in houses late at night?

Dust Fairies make a mess,
while hidden from our sight.

Fairy boys are rowdy, spitting crumbs for fun,

launching soot from slingshots,

laughing as they run.

Most fairy girls are dainty.
They work in harmony,

leaving trails of pixie dust,
that we can barely see.

The boys and girls together
play dress up games in style,
wearing capes of spider webs
that seem to stretch for miles.

A special group of fairies
comes forward when it's time,
to play their cheerful music
amid the dirt and grime.

While the dust is flying
hither, to, and fro,
fairy music follows,
everywhere they go.

Aggie tried to join them.
She belted out a song.

No one seemed to like it.
Perhaps she played too strong.

Aggie wasn't dainty.
And Aggie wasn't shy.

When she squeezed her bagpipes,
the fairy girls would sigh.

"Aggie, dearest Aggie,"
the fairy girls would chant.
"Fairies do not bellow.
You absolutely can't!"

"A graceful,
gentle fairy
would never make
that face."

Aggie tried her fairy best
to mind her P's and Q's,

keeping track of each DO NOT
and all that she should DO.

She tried to fix
her crazy hair,
and stuck
barrettes in place.

Instead of
pigtails on the top,
they drooped
into her face.

She worked to get her clothing right,
but everything went wrong.
The stocking on her left was short.
The other sock was long.

Aggie made the effort.
She gave it her best try.
Trying to be perfect,
it made her want to cry.

She'd fly away each evening,
while other fairies played.
She'd find a hidden corner,
and that is where she stayed.

She'd hug her tattered bunny,
and cry her dusty tears.
She'd whisper to him softly,
and share her little fears.

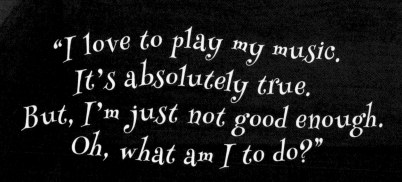

"I love to play my music.
It's absolutely true.
But, I'm just not good enough.
Oh, what am I to do?"

Dust Bunny wasn't bothered,
if Aggie missed a chord.

He sat in patient silence,
and never once looked bored.

When Aggie played her bagpipes,
a key or two she'd miss.
But the music touched her soul.
It filled her heart with bliss.

One cold night, lost in song,
she heard a clapping sound.

CLAP

CLAP CLAP

CLAP CLAP

CLAP

Just beyond the darkness,
imagine what she found.

The sad look on Aggie's face,
it sure did say a lot...
How could she be good enough,
with all that she was not?

So, Aggie grabbed her bagpipes.
Dust Bunny tagged along.
They zipped away together,
to play the band a song.

Sure enough, they welcomed her.
It was a perfect fit.

Droopy socks and crazy hair,
they didn't mind a bit.

Every night, they play 'till dawn,
not hitting every key.

It's perfect imperfection,
in blissful harmony.

If you listen close enough,
at bedtime, you might hear.
When Aggie plays her bagpipes,
it tickles in your ear.

Aggie isn't dainty.
And Aggie isn't shy.

She's not prim or proper.
She doesn't even try.

Loud and clumsy, big and bold,
so happy, wild, and free.

She's Absolutely Aggie,
just how she's meant to be!

The End.

The Writer

Michelle Eastman loves picture books so much, she decided to write her own. She is also the author of The Legend of Dust Bunnies, a Fairy's Tale. Writing for kids, and working as an elementary teacher, inspired her to develop Picture Book Pass it On, a literacy initiative providing free books to kids in need. When she is not cleaning up after Dust Fairies, she enjoys spending time with her family at their home in Waukee, Iowa.

Visit her at www.michelleeastmanbooks.com

The Illustrator

Kevin Richter has worked in various creative jobs throughout his career but has found his true passion in illustration and cartooning. He lives with his wife and their two sons in the beautiful English town of Royal Tunbridge Wells in Kent.

Visit Kev at www.kevtoon.com

CPSIA information can be obtained
at www.ICGtesting.com
Printed in the USA
LVIC06n0910291015
460064LV00001BA/1